junk

A Spectacular Tale of Trash

Written by Nicholas Day Illustrated by Tom Disbury

To Isaiah and Mila, who know a good piece of junk when they see one.

−Nicholas

For Bry, Zach, and Milo, X

−Tom

Text Copyright © 2018 Nicholas Day
Illustration Copyright © 2018 Tom Disbury
Design Copyright © 2018 Sleeping Bear Press

Sleeping Bear Press
2395 South Huron Parkway, Suite 200
Ann Arbor, MI 48104
www.sleepingbearpress.com

Printed and bound in the United States.

10 9 8 7 6 5 4 3 2 1

Library of Congress Cataloging-in-Publication Data

Names: Day, Nick (Nicholas), author. | Disbury, Tom, illustrator.
Title: Junk : a spectacular tale of trash / written by Nicholas Day ;
illustrated by Tom Disbury.
Description: Ann Arbor, MI : Sleeping Bear Press, [2018] | Summary: "Sylvia Samantha Wright
is very good at finding—she just doesn't know exactly what all her 'junk' is good for, not yet at least.
But when completely ridiculous disaster strikes, she springs into action and uses her junk
to create solutions to the town's troubles"—Provided by publisher.
Identifiers: LCCN 2018014168 | ISBN 9781585364008
Subjects: | CYAC: Refuse and refuse disposal—Fiction. | Recycling
(Waste)—Fiction. | Disasters—Fiction. | City and town life—Fiction.
Classification: LCC PZ7.1.D3944 Jun 2018 | DDC [E]—dc23
LC record available at https://lccn.loc.gov/2018014168

Sylvia Samantha Wright was very good at finding.

ON MONDAY, she found some leaky tires. And some tangled ropes that were underneath the leaky tires. And some old wood that was underneath the tangled ropes that were underneath the leaky tires.

Luckily, she had a place to put it.

And there was still enough room for the car.

"Sylvia Samantha Wright, WHY?" said her father.

"I'm working on something," said Sylvia Samantha Wright.

ON TUESDAY, she found a pack of gum with almost half the sticks still left.

Her brother did not find any gum. Her brother found reasons not to find things.

"Someone else's gum?" said her brother. "Off the sidewalk? WHY?"

"I'm working on something," said Sylvia Samantha Wright.

"Could someone work on getting me another sister, please!?" said her brother.

ON WEDNESDAY, she found some pipes no longer piping, some motors no longer motoring, and a teetering stack of paint cans with no paint.

"Let me guess," said the mayor, who lived next door.

"I'm working on something," said Sylvia Samantha Wright.

"Sure," said the mayor. "Sure you are."

ON THURSDAY, she found an abandoned collection of polka-dotted party hats from a store that was getting out of the polka-dotted party hat business.

On her way home she also found Ezekiel Mather. He was easy to find. He was walking very slowly around the block. As far as she could tell, Ezekiel Mather had spent his last eighty years walking very slowly around the block.

"Good eye," said Ezekiel Mather. "What are you working on?"

Sylvia Samantha Wright had never heard Ezekiel Mather ask anyone what they were working on before. She'd never heard him say anything to anyone before.

She swallowed. Then she said something she'd never said to anyone before.

"I don't know," she said.

Ezekiel Mather smiled.

She had never seen him smile before, either.

"That's the best part," he said. "The part before you know."

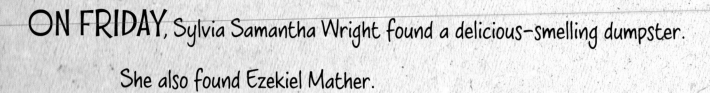

ON FRIDAY, Sylvia Samantha Wright found a delicious-smelling dumpster.

She also found Ezekiel Mather.

"Good eye," said Ezekiel Mather. He found a ladder and held it steady.

Sylvia Samantha Wright climbed up and peeked inside. "The whole thing," she reported, "is full of half-rotten bananas."

REDUCE
REUSE
RECYCLE

Ezekiel Mather laughed so hard his shoulders shook. He laughed so hard Sylvia Samantha Wright had to hold on tight.

She didn't mind. She had never seen Ezekiel Mather laugh before.

"What are you going to do," he said, "with a dumpster full of

HALF-ROTTEN BANANAS?"

"I don't know," said Sylvia Samantha Wright. "But I think this is the part before I know."

ON SATURDAY, the water tower sprung a few leaks.

"I've got this," said the mayor, putting buckets under the leaks.

The water filled up the buckets and swept away the town playground.

"I've got this," said the mayor, floating away on the tire swing.

The floating playground took out the main power line for the town.

"I've got this," said the mayor, logrolling on a downed utility pole.

The power outage shorted the security system of the zoo's Larger-Sized Animal House, opening the cages of three hippopotamuses, seven orangutans, an unknown number of capybaras, and one Asian elephant, who pulled up the flagpole outside City Hall and began using it as a baton.

"I DO NOT HAVE THIS," said the mayor, clinging to the flagpole.

ON SUNDAY, Sylvia Samantha Wright walked over to City Hall.

She walked up to the mayor.

"I'm here to help," said Sylvia Samantha Wright.

The mayor looked down at the leaky tires and the tangled ropes and the old wood. She looked at the pack of gum with almost half the sticks still left. She looked at the pipes no longer piping, the motors no longer motoring, and the teetering stack of paint cans with no paint. She looked at the abandoned polka-dotted party hats.

The mayor scratched her head.

"I've got this," said Sylvia Samantha Wright.

Upon closer inspection, she found there were exactly as many sticks of gum as there were leaks.

It turns out that if you have a pile of pipes, some motors connected to nothing at all, and a whole lot of paint cans with no paint, you also have a whole lot of wind turbines.

The new playground was a vast improvement.

"But what about," said the mayor, "the three hippopotamuses, seven orangutans, an unknown number of capybaras, and one Asian elephant?"

"For that," said Sylvia Samantha Wright, "I'll need YOUR help."

The escaped animals were all herbivores.

And just as Sylvia Samantha Wright suspected, all of them decided that 43 wheelbarrows of three-quarters-rotten bananas were an excellent reason to return to the Larger-Sized Animal House.

The residents of the town looked at the dripless water tower.

They looked at the whirling, electricity-generating wind turbines.

They looked at the wondrous new playground.

Then they looked at the polka-dotted party hats.

"Sylvia Samantha Wright, WHY?" they said.

She looked at Ezekiel Mather.

"Do you want to say it?" she asked.

"For the PARTY, of course," said Ezekiel Mather.

ON MONDAY, Sylvia Samantha Wright found a rusty bucket with just the right number of holes.